FOR MY MOM, WHO FIRST ENCOURAGED ME TO PURSUE
MY PASSION FOR WRITING AND HAS ALWAYS HELPED ME
TURN LEMONS INTO LEMONADE. —J.L.B.D.

FOR GRANDMA JOAN AND GRANDMA DEE —L.R.

A NOTE FROM THE AUTHOR:

In 2015, my husband, Ricky, was diagnosed with a brain tumor.
Despite everything he's faced, he continues to inspire our family and many others
with his courage and strength. In honor of him, as well as the brain tumor patients
and childhood cancer patients we've met on this journey, a gray ribbon and a
gold ribbon have been included in the illustrations to raise awareness
and show support for all those affected by these diagnoses.

STERLING CHILDREN'S BOOKS
New York

An Imprint of Sterling Publishing Co., Inc.
1166 Avenue of the Americas
New York, NY 10036

ISBN 978-1-4549-2381-7

Distributed in Canada by Sterling Publishing Co., Inc.
c/o Canadian Manda Group, 664 Annette Street
Toronto, Ontario M6S 2C8, Canada
Distributed in the United Kingdom by GMC Distribution Services
Castle Place, 166 High Street, Lewes, East Sussex BN7 1XU, England
Distributed in Australia by NewSouth Books
University of New South Wales, Sydney, NSW 2052, Australia

For information about custom editions, special sales, and premium and corporate purchases,
please contact Sterling Special Sales at 800-805-5489 or specialsales@sterlingpublishing.com.

Manufactured in the United States of America

Lot #:
2 4 6 8 10 9 7 5 3
03/19

sterlingpublishing.com

When Grandma Gives You A Lemon Tree

WRITTEN BY
JAMIE L. B. DEENIHAN

ILLUSTRATED BY
LORRAINE ROCHA

STERLING CHILDREN'S BOOKS
New York

You were hoping for one of these:

But, surprise! It's a . . .

. . . LEMON TREE.

What should you do when Grandma gives
you a lemon tree for your birthday?

First of all, act excited.

Your face should
look like this:

Not this:

And definitely
not this:

Next, say something polite. Try:
"Thank you. Just what I . . . needed?"

Keep smiling until Grandma leaves (or falls asleep),
and do not harm your lemon tree.

DON'T:

Drop it off a bridge.

Tie it to your birthday balloons.

Play ding dong ditch the lemon tree.

Now, listen closely. This is important.

Place your lemon tree in a sunny spot.

Be careful not to overwater.

And prepare for battle against intruders.

When winter arrives, keep your lemon tree warm.

Then wait.

And wait.

And wait some more.

Once the snow melts, it's time to bring your lemon tree back outside.

WELL DONE!

Sure, you can decorate your lemon tree.

Or hide behind it. Come out, come out, wherever you are!

But you know what's even more fun?

picking Lemons!

Woo-Hoo!

Pick them. Slice them. Squeeze them.
Come on—squeeze, squeeze, squeeze-a-roo!

Ta-da! Now you have lemon juice.

You didn't think I'd just leave you with lemon juice, did you?

Of course not.

Remember those gifts you were hoping for?

It's good you're staying focused.

Gather these items:

1. Lemon juice.

2. Water.

3. A pinch (or handful) of sugar.

Recipes ❦

Classic Lemonade

Ingredients: 4 lemons, 4 cups water, 1/3 cup sugar, ice

Squeeze lemons. Add water. Add sugar. Mix until sugar is dissolved. Pour over ice. Enjoy!

4. Flashy lemonade stand.

Cue a dazzling smile and . . .

...KA-CHING!

Count your cash and head to the store.

Welcome MEGASTORE

Pear

Garden
Today only!
ALL plants on
SALE!

ROBOT
Dogs

Now you can finally buy
exactly what you want.

Something you can really enjoy.

AND SHARE WITH OTHERS. TOO.